MARY-KATE & ASHLEY

Starring in

Passport to Paris™

Novelization by Wendy Wax

Based on the teleplay by
Elizabeth Kruger and Craig Shapiro

A PARACHUTE PRESS BOOK

PARACHUTE PRESS

Parachute Publishing, L.L.C.
156 Fifth Avenue
New York, NY 10010

 DUALSTAR PUBLICATIONS

Dualstar Publications
c/o Thorne and Company
A Professional Law Corporation
1801 Century Park East
Los Angeles, CA 90067

Troll Communications L.L.C.
100 Corporate Drive
Mahwah, NJ 07430

Book created and produced by Parachute Publishing, L.L.C.,
in cooperation with Dualstar Publishing, a division of
Dualstar Entertainment Group, Inc.

ISBN 1-57351-008-4

First Printing: October 2000
Printed in the United States of America

10 9 8 7 6 5 4 3 2 1

CHAPTER ONE

"You're staring, Ally," Melanie Porter said to her twin sister. She bit into her sandwich. It was another beautiful day in Southern California, and everyone was having lunch outside. There was a buzz of excitement about spring break next week.

"I wish they'd ask us to the Spring Fling dance," Allison Porter, better known as Ally, said dreamily. She gazed at Shane and Kyle, two of Northwood Junior High's most popular guys. Shane had sun-streaked blond hair and freckles. Kyle had brown hair that hung in his face. They sat one table over.

"They are *so* hot," Ally said. She twisted a strand of blond hair around one finger and sighed.

Melanie had to agree with her sister. Shane and Kyle were totally adorable—especially Kyle. "Let's sit with them," she suggested. "I mean, we're all in social studies together, and there's room at their table."

"Not anymore," Ally said. "Look."

Melanie watched as Helene and Darlene, two

perky cheerleaders, strolled up to the boys' table and set down their trays. Her big blue eyes narrowed.

"We'll never get near Shane and Kyle with Tweedledum and Tweedledumber around," said Melanie. "Unless..."

"Unless what?" Ally asked, looking at her sister.

"If you can't beat 'em, mess with their heads," Melanie said, her eyes twinkling.

Ally grinned. "I'm all for it!" She pulled a tiny mirror and a tube of lip gloss out of her bag. "Let me just do a quick touch-up."

Melanie blew out her breath in a sigh. Ally was much more into makeup than she was. Not that Melanie didn't wear a touch of lip gloss herself—but the inside of Ally's locker looked like a cosmetics store, with a makeup rack on the door and cutouts from fashion magazines pasted everywhere. The inside of Melanie's locker, on the other hand, was covered with music posters. A stack of CDs sat on the top shelf.

As soon as the two girls stood up, they were bombarded with hellos and waves.

"Cool hair clips, Ally," a petite redhead called out.

"Thanks," Ally said. She always got compliments on her fashion sense. Today she wore a black T-shirt with a white batik print and a hip skirt.

Melanie was sporting a cool blue three-quarter T-shirt and capri pants. Both girls wore choker-style necklaces and high platform sandals.

Melanie led the way toward Shane and Kyle's table.

When they were about five feet away, Shane stood up, holding his empty Jell-O bowl. "Kyle, let's snag some more lime slime," he said.

"Dude!" said Kyle. He stood up, too.

"Back in a minute," Shane said to the cheerleaders.

Melanie held out an arm to stop Ally. "Perfect timing! Here's our chance," she whispered. Ally nodded.

"Helene, you are so much more popular than I am," Darlene said as soon as the two cheerleaders were alone. "I mean, yes, I'm cool. But you're way cooler." She took a bite of meatloaf.

Melanie rolled her eyes. "Oh, brother! Okay, let's do it," she whispered. Then she said in a loud voice, "It's super top secret, Ally!" Out of the corner of her eye she checked to see if Darlene and Helene were listening.

She had to hold back a grin. Darlene and Helene were craning their necks to hear what she would say next.

"C'mon, Mel," Ally begged, giving Melanie a secret wink. "I promise not to tell anybody."

"Well," Melanie said. She leaned closer to Ally. "I heard that five kids went home sick today after eating the meatloaf. The meat was so bad it had E. coli *and* F. coli."

"Ewwwww!" Darlene and Helene yelled, spitting pieces of meatloaf back onto their plates.

"Wow. Did it have little brown worms?" Ally asked.

"No," Melanie said. "Those white squishy ones— like this one over here." She leaned over and pulled a nasty-looking worm off Helene's plate, dangling it in the air.

"Aaaahhhh!" Darlene and Helene screamed, racing toward the bathroom. On the way they passed Shane and Kyle, who were returning with more green Jell-O.

Laughing, Ally and Melanie gave each other high fives.

"Hey, Melanie," Kyle said to Ally as the boys walked up.

"Hey, Ally," Shane said to Melanie.

"Hey!" Ally said, ignoring the name mix-up.

"*I'm* Melanie. That's Ally," Melanie informed them as she sat down.

"Oh, right," Shane said, sitting next to her.

"Worm?" Ally offered the boys a bag of candy worms.

"Cool! Gross-out candy," Kyle said, sitting next to Ally.

"You guys are all right," Shane said.

Ally and Melanie exchanged sly smiles. All right! Melanie cheered silently.

After lunch, Shane, Kyle, Melanie, and Ally walked to Mr. Harper's social studies class together. Mr. Harper was short, with a graying beard and mustache, and glasses.

"In 1805," Mr. Harper began, "Napoleon upgraded the sewers so he could claim France had the most advanced water system in the world." He droned on and on in a monotone.

Melanie pulled out her French homework and began to copy the vocabulary words into her notebook. She knew Ally was doing the same thing, two seats in front of her. This way, they wouldn't have to do it when they got home.

She glanced up as a piece of folded paper landed on her desk. Unfolding it, she saw that it was from Ally. "KYLE IS LOOKING AT YOU," it read.

She glanced up at Kyle, who sat in the first row, and caught his eye. He finished folding a note and kicked the desk of the boy behind him. He jerked his head toward Melanie.

Melanie's heart beat faster as the note made its way toward her. Did it say what she hoped it said?

When it finally reached her desk, Melanie reached over to grab it. But a big hand beat her to it. She glanced up, startled.

"Hmmm. What have we here?" Mr. Harper said, unfolding the note. "'Mel, how about Shane and me take you and Ally to Spring Fling dance next Saturday night?'" he read aloud.

Melanie felt her cheeks grow warm. The class laughed.

"Well, Melanie, Ally," Mr. Harper said. "What do you have to say for yourselves?"

Melanie picked up her pen, wrote one word in her notebook, tore out the page, and handed it to Mr. Harper. Ally did the same thing.

"'Definitely!' 'Definitely!'" he read from each note.

Everyone laughed again. Melanie's cheeks were burning by now, but she couldn't help grinning. If she had to get caught passing notes, she might as well do it in style!

Brrring! Saved by the bell!

Melanie and Ally grabbed their books and raced toward the door. "All right!" they both screamed as they burst out into the hall. Spring break was here—and they had dates for Spring Fling!

CHAPTER TWO

That evening, Melanie and Ally wolfed down their dinner. Then they waited impatiently for their parents to finish theirs. It was the twins' job to clear the table and wash the dishes.

"Where's the fire?" their mom asked suspiciously. She was tall with short brown hair.

"No fire, Mom," Melanie said. "We just have some spring break calendar work to do."

"What ever happened to homework?" their dad asked. He was a little taller than their mother and had dark brown hair.

"It's done, Dad," Melanie said. "We did math during science, science during English...."

"...and the rest in social studies," Ally said, standing up. She couldn't wait any longer. "That class is so S and C."

"What?" Their parents looked puzzled.

"Snooze and cruise," Ally explained. "Personally, I think Mr. Harper has a short-guy complex. Napoleon this, Napoleon that."

"Right. I know Napoleon conquered Europe and crowned himself emperor and stuff, but hello. The guy crashed and burned in Russia," Melanie said.

"Tanked at Waterloo," Ally added.

"Talk about a Bore War," Melanie said, rolling her eyes.

"If I were running the world, there'd be no wars. That's for sure," Ally concluded. "Just pool parties."

Their mom gave their dad a hopeless look.

After dinner, Ally put on her telephone headset. So did Melanie. Then the girls washed the dishes, each of them yakking to a friend. The chores seemed like no problem when you were talking to a friend at the same time.

This headset makes life so much easier! Ally thought.

When they were done, they went up to their bedroom and got down to business.

"Spring break is going to be awesome," Ally said. "Margie's beach party is next Thursday." She uncapped a pen and began to write in their plans on the Backstreet Boys calendar that hung between their beds. Behind it, the wallpaper was pink and white, as was most of the room. Music posters and fashion ads adorned the walls.

"Friday is Hannah's pool party," Melanie said.

"Then, Saturday is the Spring Fling dance," Ally said. She sighed happily. "With gorgeous Shane!"

"And perfect Kyle," Melanie said. "I wish spring break could last forever."

"Knock, knock," their dad called from the hallway. A moment later, he poked his head in. "You're supposed to say 'Who's there?'"

"Dad," Ally said kindly, "we're a little old for knock-knock jokes."

"It's totally Barney," Melanie added.

"Then I guess you're too old for presents," their mom said from behind him. She was holding two identical small boxes. She shrugged and turned to leave.

Presents?

"No! Wait!" Melanie called.

"You're never too old for presents," Ally added.

They grabbed the boxes and eagerly opened them.

Ally stared in confusion at what was inside hers. "A passport and a camera?" she said.

"Where are we going?" Melanie asked.

"Paris," their mom said, handing them a thick maroon guidebook and an English/French dictionary.

Ally's mouth fell open. Then she grabbed Melanie by the arms and began dancing around in circles with her.

"We're going to Paris!" she yelled. "High five!"

"Just think—a spring break filled with culture," their dad said, smiling.

"Spring break?" Ally said, stopping mid-high five. Uh-oh!

"But we've got plans all week," Melanie said.

"You're leaving very early Sunday morning," their dad said. "For a week. So you'd better start packing."

"Nooo!" the girls groaned together.

"We'll miss the dance," Ally said. She sank down on Melanie's bed. This was a major disaster!

"Sorry, but the tickets are nonrefundable," their mother said. She patted Ally's shoulder. "Anyway, it's about time you learned that there's more to life than call waiting and sales at Bloomingdale's. Cheer up. It's going to be great!"

"You can practice your French, Ally," their dad said. The phone in the hall rang, and he left the room.

"You'll be staying with Grandpa Edward," their mother told them.

Grandpa Edward? Ally winced. This trip was sounding worse and worse!

"But he's so strict," Melanie complained. "You might as well send us to prison."

"It would be a lot cheaper than Paris," Ally pointed out.

"Look," their mother said sympathetically. "I know he's not great with you kids, but—"

"That's like saying the *Titanic*'s not great with icebergs," Ally muttered.

Their mom sighed. "Girls," she said, sitting between them on Melanie's bed. "Your grandfather loves you. He's just busy, and often forgets to show it. Being the ambassador to France is a very demanding job." She stood up and looked at them. "I'm sorry about the dance, but there will be others. Trust me."

There was a long silence after she left the room. "I hope she's right about those other dances," Melanie said at last.

"It sure won't be fun breaking the news to Shane and Kyle," Ally said. Then she had a horrible thought. "Oh, no! They'll probably end up going to the dance with Helene and Darlene."

"Forget Kyle and Shane," Melanie said. Ally could tell she was trying to convince herself. "Who needs them, anyway? They couldn't even tell us apart."

"Maybe you're right," Ally said uncertainly. "It's just that...I thought Shane was going to be my first real boyfriend. What if we don't ever get asked out again until we're twenty?"

"We'll blame our parents," Melanie said.

Ally cracked a smile. "Well, I guess we'd better start packing."

"That's the attitude," Melanie said. She jumped up, pulled out her suitcase from the closet and began tossing CDs into it.

Ally walked over to the open closet and studied her clothes. Hmmm. Which ones were the most sophisticated? It would be awful to go to Paris without the perfect outfits.

As she began pulling out tops and skirts, excitement bubbled up inside her. It was a major drag that they were missing the Spring Fling, but...Paris! They were really going to Paris!

CHAPTER THREE

It was a long plane ride. Melanie and Ally spent the first half talking, reading magazines, and watching a movie. Just as they finally drifted off to sleep, the pilot woke them up with an announcement: "Ladies and gentlemen, please fasten your seat belts as we make our final descent into Paris. Don't forget to set your watches six hours ahead. It is now six P.M. local time."

By the time Melanie was fully awake, they had already gotten their passports stamped, gone through customs, and had a porter help them with their luggage.

At last Melanie spotted a dark-haired man in a suit, holding up a sign that read "MELANIE AND ALLISON PORTER."

"That's us!" Melanie said, but the man was too busy talking into his cell phone to notice them.

"Hello?" Ally said, waving her hands in front of his face.

An annoyed look flashed across the man's face.

"I'll get back to you on that," he said into the phone. Then he flipped it shut and turned to the girls.

"I'm Jeremy Bluff," he said. "Special assistant to the ambassador. Now, which of you is which?"

"I'm Beavis," Melanie said.

"And I'm Butthead," Ally said.

Jeremy gave them a withering look.

"Tough crowd," Melanie whispered to Ally as Jeremy herded them into a limousine.

"To the embassy, Jacques," he said to the driver, and they were off, speeding through the city of Paris.

Tired from traveling, the girls gazed out the windows and took in the sites with awe.

"Photo op!" Melanie cried. She grabbed her camera from her blue knapsack and snapped a picture of a big white marble arch. She knew from her guidebook that it was called the Arc de Triomphe.

"This street is the Champs-Élysées," Ally said, pulling her camera out of her pink backpack. "The most major shopping street in the world!"

Finally, they arrived. "This is the Place de la Concorde," Jeremy told them. Two guards in uniform stepped aside as tall, majestic gates swung open and the limousine pulled into the courtyard of the American Embassy.

"Wow!" Melanie said, opening her door. The big old building was very impressive.

"Double wow!" Ally said as they entered an echoing front hall. It had a high ceiling covered with fancy plaster carvings, and a shiny black-and-white-tiled floor. A wide marble staircase swept upward at the back of the room.

"For a civil servant, Grandpa's doing all right," Melanie whispered.

"Are those my granddaughters?" said a gruff voice from above.

Melanie gulped as her tall, silver-haired, elegantly dressed grandfather strode down the staircase. Grandpa Edward's hawk nose and piercing stare had terrified her when she was little. She was still a little nervous around him.

"Hi, Grandpa," the girls said together.

"Welcome to Paris," their grandfather said. He gave Melanie and Ally stiff hugs, and stepped back to look at them. "It's been too long. Almost fifteen months since I've been to the States. Since I took this assignment, I never seem to have any free time."

Melanie pursed her lips. Grandpa Edward hadn't had any free time before he took the ambassador's job, either.

"François," Grandpa Edward said to a black-coated butler who had appeared at his side. "My granddaughters, Allison and Melanie."

He got it wrong. *Oh, boy,* Melanie thought. *Off to a great start! "I'm* Melanie. *She's* Ally," she corrected.

"Charmed, mesdemoiselles," François said with a bow. His French accent was very thick.

Just then, a man with a handlebar mustache bustled into the foyer. He wore a chef's hat and white gloves.

"Henri, meet my granddaughters," Grandpa Edward said. "They just arrived from the United States."

Henri bowed quickly. "Honored. Enthralled," he said with a touch of sarcasm. "I am Henri, the chef, and, no, I do not have any hot dogs or peanut butter. Now, excusez-moi, I have a soufflé just moments from disaster. Ay-ay-ay!"

Ally nudged Melanie as Henri scuttled away, muttering to himself. "Cuckoo," she whispered. Melanie nodded.

While François took their luggage upstairs, Grandpa Edward led the girls and Jeremy into an impressive study. Their grandfather seated himself at a huge oak desk. There was a large American flag behind him. Melanie and Ally perched on a beige leather couch, while Jeremy remained standing.

"Unfortunately, girls," Grandpa Edward said, "I have a very busy schedule this week, so I won't be able to chaperone you around the city."

"It figures," Melanie whispered to Ally.

"My assistant, Jeremy, will be happy to act as your guide," Grandpa Edward said. He handed Jeremy a black folder.

"What? Me?" Jeremy said, looking horrified. "But, Mr. Ambassador, my work on the Clean Water Treaty—I've drafted a position paper for your review."

"I already have staff working on the Clean Water Treaty," Grandpa Edward said irritably. "Your responsibility this week is Allison and Melanie."

"But—" Jeremy pleaded.

"It's all been arranged," Grandpa Edward said. "You'll find a full schedule for each day there in the folder."

"Yes, sir," Jeremy said stiffly.

"Great," Ally whispered. "We're stuck with Borezilla."

"At least we'll have fun torturing him this week," Melanie whispered back. "Maybe we can loosen him up a little."

"Him?" Ally sounded doubtful. "That's a tall order."

"Girls, let me remind you that in France you are representatives of the American people," Grandpa Edward said sternly. "I expect you to comport yourselves like ladies. Is that clear?"

Melanie and Ally nodded solemnly. *Sure—whatever "comport" means,* Melanie thought.

"Now François will show you around," Grandpa Edward said, ringing a bell on his desk. A moment later François stepped in.

François took the girls on a brief tour of the embassy. They saw the library, the drawing room, and the kitchen, which had a separate entrance for deliveries. All the rooms had high ceilings, potted plants, elegant statues, and beautiful rugs.

"I'm impressed," Melanie said, as François led them up the stairs.

"Your room is to the left," François said.

The girls raced to the door and flung it open.

The room was at least three times the size of their bedroom at home, with two four-poster beds, an antique vanity table, a marble fireplace, and a balcony that overlooked the courtyard. In the distance they could see the Tuileries Gardens.

"Cool!" Ally said.

"Awesome!" Melanie said. She gazed around the room. "For a museum, that is."

Ally nodded. "It does need a little...something, doesn't it?"

The twins faced each other, grinning. "Let's get to work!" Melanie said.

CHAPTER FOUR

"Done!" Melanie said. She stepped back to admire her alphabetized CDs, which took up four shelves. A poster of her favorite band hung above her bed, and the boom box she'd brought from home was blasting.

She danced over to the vanity, where Ally had just finished setting up her makeup and lip gloss collection, and picked up a dark eye pencil.

"I thought you didn't like wearing makeup," Ally shouted over the music. She watched her sister draw a handlebar mustache on her face in front of the mirror.

"I am Henri!" Melanie said, in a bad French accent. "Ze Americain cooking tastes like ze ca-ca poo-poo. I will not serve ze hot diggity doggies!"

They both burst out laughing. Ally jumped up on her bed and started to dance. Then Melanie jumped up on her bed, and the two of them boogied to the blaring music, until—

"What is all this noise?" a man's voice roared.

Ally jumped and turned toward the door. Grandpa Edward stood there, glaring at them.

"You mean the Scapegoats?" Melanie yelled, pointing at the boom box. She went to turn it down.

"I mean my granddaughters," Grandpa Edward said. "This behavior is entirely unacceptable here!"

Ally swallowed hard. Whoops!

"Now," Grandpa Edward continued sternly. "Tonight dinner is being served at twenty hundred hours, due to your late arrival, but usually it's served promptly at nineteen hundred hours. You are to dress appropriately. Is that understood?"

The girls nodded, not daring to look at each other.

Grandpa Edward looked at the music and fashion posters, and then at Melanie's fake mustache. He shook his head and left.

"Yikes!" Melanie said when he left. "Here for an hour and already in trouble."

"Maybe dinner will be more laid back," Ally said hopefully.

But it wasn't. Dinner was a formal affair with fine china and crystal at a long, rectangular table. Candelabras lit up the room. The girls wore black dresses with pearls.

Grandpa Edward sat the head of the table, with

his granddaughters to his left and Jeremy to his right. The rest of the table was unused.

Ally was starving. The last thing she'd eaten was a soggy muffin on the plane that morning. She reached for a breadstick and bit hungrily into it.

Kaaa-runch! All eyes turned to her.

Ally shrank under the weight of all those stares. "Sorry," she said, putting the half-eaten breadstick back in the basket.

Melanie kicked her under the table as Grandpa Edward raised his eyebrows. Luckily, they were saved by Henri, who entered the room through a swinging door.

"The first course: Escargots Henri," he announced, "served at precisely one hundred seventy-nine degrees, or all is lost."

"Thank you, Henri," Grandpa Edward said, as François began to serve. "Eat up, girls."

"What is this stuff?" Ally whispered to Melanie as she examined the stuff on her plate.

"Beats me," Melanie said, "but I'm hungry." She took a tiny bite.

Ally watched closely. A look of rapture spread across Melanie's face. "Delish!" she murmured.

Ally put a forkful of the stuff into her mouth. It was amazing! Garlicky, buttery—yum! She closed her eyes with pleasure. Then she speared another of the little lumps with her fork.

"I had no idea you girls liked snails," Grandpa Edward said, looking pleased.

Ally practically choked. *Snails?*

"Yah!" the girls yelled, flicking the slimy snails off their forks.

Splat! Like two alien eyes, the snails whacked into François's forehead, just as he was serving Jeremy.

"Ooops." Melanie gave Grandpa Edward an apologetic look.

Unfazed, François wiped off the snails with a handkerchief. "In a butter and garlic sauce, if I am not mistaken," he added.

The girls put down their forks and waited hungrily for the next course.

Ten minutes later, Henri came in and announced the second course: "Pâté de fois gras."

"And that would be...?" Ally asked nervously.

"Ze poached liver of ze force-fed goose," Henri answered proudly as François began to serve.

Liver? Blech! Ally was starting to get worried. Would they be able to eat *anything* in France?

"No thanks, I'm allergic to that," Melanie said, waving François away.

"Me, too," Ally said. "It's a twin thing."

Their grandfather shook his head with disapproval.

Ally bit her lip. She was getting the feeling it was going to be a long week.

Later that night, Melanie and Ally lay in bed. Ally clapped her hands over her stomach as a loud growling sound came from it.

"I'm starving," Melanie complained. "I can't sleep on an empty stomach."

"I feel your pain," Ally said. "But what are we going to do? Order a pizza?"

Just then, Melanie's stomach let out a rumble so loud Ally heard it across the room. "I guess we'll have to," Melanie said, turning on the light.

Using the phone book, the English/French dictionary, and the phone, they managed to order a pizza. Then they tiptoed down to the embassy kitchen with their French phrase book to meet the delivery boy at the back entrance.

But when they reached the kitchen, Ally saw a light on. She froze, her heart pounding.

"Nobody in zis embassy would order from Le Pizza Hut," Henri was shouting. "Nobody!"

"Oh, no," Melanie groaned. "I didn't think they'd

get here this fast. What do we do now?"

There was nothing they could do but tough it out, Ally realized. "Come on," she said. She checked her French phrase book one last time. Then, squaring her shoulders, she entered the kitchen.

They found Henri, dressed in a nightshirt and nightcap, arguing with a delivery boy in a Le Pizza Hut shirt.

"Mi saucisse, mi saucisson?" Ally asked the delivery boy coolly. "That means 'half pepperoni, half sausage,'" she whispered to Henri, who stared at her with horror.

"Oui!" said the delivery boy, sounding relieved.

"Merci!" Ally said, taking the pizza box. The pizza smelled great. She handed the delivery boy some French money. Then she gave Henri a sweet smile and sailed past him. She could feel his glare burning into the back of her neck, but she didn't even slow down.

Melanie followed. "Don't forget to give him a big tip, Henri," she called over her shoulder, as she and Ally headed toward the stairs.

CHAPTER FIVE

"Last one to the Louvre is a rotten baguette," Melanie said the next morning as she climbed out of the limousine. She was wearing a blue-green tank top, jeans, and a blue bandanna. Ally wore a pink tank top, a light blue skirt, and a flowered headband. They both wore sandals.

The girls raced down the street toward the grand museum.

"Wait, girls!" Jeremy called, grabbing the schedule. He stepped out of the car, tripped, and fell sprawling into a puddle.

Melanie grabbed Ally's hand and pulled her into the busy street.

Honk! Honk!

Melanie spun around and spotted two mopeds zooming toward her and Ally. "Yikes!" she yelped, and jumped out of the way.

The mopeds circled around and came to a stop. The drivers looked about fourteen. And, Melanie noticed with a surge of interest, they were *very* cute.

"Vraiment désolé, je ne vous ai pas vu," one of them said, looking at Ally. He had green eyes and a broad, mischievous smile. Light, wavy hair poked out of his helmet.

"What did he say?" Melanie asked Ally.

"Who cares?" Ally said, dreamily.

The boy pulled a red rose from one of many bouquets in his saddlebag and tossed it to Ally.

The other boy was a bit taller than his friend, with dark brown hair and eyes. He tossed a yellow rose to Melanie and smiled. Then the two of them rode off.

Wow, Melanie thought. *That was so romantic and French!*

"Pinch me," Ally murmured.

Melanie pinched her sister.

"Ow!" Ally yelled. "That hurt!"

Just then, Jeremy reached them, looking muddy and annoyed.

"You're a mess, Jeremy," Ally said, giggling. "You're going to give Americans a bad rap."

"What does Les Fleurs d'Amour mean, Jeremy?" Melanie asked.

"'Flowers of love,'" Jeremy muttered in a grumpy voice.

"That's what was stenciled on those two boys'

saddlebags, Ally," Melanie told her sister.

"Come on, girls," Jeremy said impatiently. "We have a busy day."

They headed into the Louvre museum. "Hello, and welcome," said their tour guide, a middle-aged woman with a gray bun and a strange accent. "The Louvre is home to nearly ten miles of halls, four hundred rooms, and over one million works of art. In fact, if you were to view each work of art for just one minute, it would take you four months to get through the museum." She led them into a huge room lined with paintings.

"Four months?" Ally whispered, sounding horrified. "But we only have a week!"

Melanie and Ally were surprised at how much they enjoyed wandering through the Louvre—at least, for the first half hour. But after three hours...

"Two thousand three hundred and sixty paintings," Melanie said wearily.

"Eight hundred and forty-seven sculptures," Ally said, rolling her eyes.

"Forty-six," Melanie corrected her. "That last one was a security guard."

Melanie heaved a sigh of relief when Jeremy announced that it was lunchtime. He led them to an outdoor café. "Go ahead and order," he told the girls as they took their seats. "I've got to make some business calls." He headed inside.

A waitress came up to their table. "Vous voulez commander?"

"Huh?" Melanie said.

"Would you like to order?" the waitress asked in English.

"Deux poissons, s'il vous plaît," Ally said in her best French. The waitress nodded and left.

"Do you know what you ordered?" Melanie said, impressed.

"Oui," Ally said. She tossed her hair. "It's about time I start using my French. Ms. Pierre says I'm a natural."

Minutes later, a plate of cold fish was placed in front of them. Ally looked confused.

"Wait, this isn't a soda," she called after the waitress. "I didn't order this."

Melanie grinned. "A natural, huh?"

"Excuse me, girls, but perhaps I can help," said a pretty woman who was sitting at the next table. She had long auburn hair, blue eyes, and a French accent.

Ally showed her what she'd ordered on the menu.

"You ordered 'poisson,'" the woman explained.

"That means 'fish.' The word for 'drink' is 'boisson.'"

"Nice going, Madame Croissant," Melanie said, giggling.

The woman explained the mix-up to the waitress, who took the fish away in a huff.

"I'm Brigitte," the woman said, smiling.

"I'm Melanie, and this is Ally," Melanie said.

"Hey, you're Brigitte—the supermodel!" Ally said, with a sudden gasp of recognition.

"She is not!" Melanie said. She turned to examine the woman closely. Brigitte did look awfully familiar. "Or—is she? I mean, are you?"

Brigitte looked amused. "I'm afraid so," she confessed.

"Oh my gosh!" Ally and Melanie said together.

"You were on the April cover of *Très Chic* magazine," Ally gushed. "In the Jean-Paul Gaultier one-piece."

"Don't tell me you spend all day with your nose buried in the fashion mags," Brigitte said.

"Not *all* day," Melanie said. "She breaks it up with some boy-scoping and mall-trawling."

Brigitte laughed. "When I was your age, I was exactly the same way," she said. "So, is this your first trip to Paris?"

The girls nodded.

"Well, it's a magical city," Brigitte said. "Full of adventure and romance, the world's best shopping and the world's cutest boys."

"Do *you* have a boyfriend?" Ally asked Brigitte.

"Ally!" Melanie said, kicking her sister.

"It's okay, Melanie," Brigitte said. "As it happens, I travel a lot for work. There's not a lot of time for boyfriends."

The waitress returned with two Diet Cokes.

"Merci," Ally said. Then she added something else in French.

The waitress looked insulted and hurried away.

"*Now* what did you say?" Melanie asked, rolling her eyes.

"I thought I said 'I like your perfume.'"

"Ally, I'm afraid you just told her she stinks," Brigitte said. The three of them burst out laughing.

Brigitte looked at her watch. "I'm late for a fitting, girls," she said, quickly paying her bill. "I'm doing a photo shoot in the Jardin du Luxembourg on Wednesday."

The girls watched her get into a taxi. "Ally, be careful where you use that French," she called. "And remember, this is Paris. Have fun!"

"All right, girls," Jeremy said, returning to the table. "Time to hit the rest of the museums."

"Museums?" Ally said. "As in…more than one?"

"But we haven't eaten yet," Melanie complained.

"Remember the schedule," said Jeremy, waving the piece of paper at them. He left money for the diet sodas on the table.

The girls were starving all afternoon. When they got back to the embassy and discovered that dinner was calves' brains with mushrooms, Melanie felt like screaming. Oh, well. At least there was salad.

"So, what did you girls learn today?" Grandpa Edward asked at dinner.

"Learn?" Ally and Melanie said at the same time.

"Jinx!" Ally said quickly.

Melanie grinned and was silent.

"Girls," Grandpa Edward said, looking annoyed. "What is going on?"

"I just jinxed her, Grandpa," Ally explained. "Don't you know about jinxing? She can't talk until someone says her name."

"Gee, what a shame," Jeremy muttered. He turned to the ambassador. "Sir, I was wondering if you've had an opportunity to review my paper on the Clean Water Treaty."

"Felanie, Relanie, Telanie, Selanie," Ally teased her sister.

"Melanie!" Jeremy shouted, glaring at Ally.

"Thanks!" Melanie said, her grin widening.

Jeremy tried to calm down. "As I was saying, sir—"

"Jeremy, we've been over this," Grandpa Edward said. "Friday night is not your concern."

"What's happening Friday night?" Melanie asked.

"The embassy is hosting a banquet for the French foreign minister and his wife," Grandpa Edward explained. "You girls will get to see how diplomacy works firsthand."

"Sounds like *Snorezilla: The Sequel*," Ally muttered.

Secretly, Melanie agreed with her sister, but she didn't say anything.

François filled her glass. "Grape juice with dinner?" she said, and gulped it down.

"That's not grape juice," Francois said. "It's…"

But Melanie had already spit it all over her plate.

"It's wine," François continued calmly. "A fine Beaujolais, if I'm not mistaken."

Grandpa Edward looked at Melanie and just shook his head.

"Why can't he be like other grandfathers?" Ally asked as the girls lay in bed that night. "A sweet old guy who sits in a rocking chair, brings us gifts, and tells us how smart and funny we are."

"Face it," Melanie said. "We don't have a grandfather. We have an ambassador."

"The best thing that's happened to us so far is nearly being run over by those French boys," Ally said sadly.

Melanie yawned. "For once, you and I agree."

"Maybe we can see them again," Ally said.

"Hello?" Melanie said. "There's, like, a zillion people here. What'll we do? Look up 'Cute Parisian boys driving mopeds' in the yellow pages?"

"No—we'll look up Les Fleurs d'Amour," Ally said. "I bet it's a flower store, don't you?"

Melanie bolted upright. "That's the name that was on their bags! A flower store!" Leaping out of bed, she threw her arms around her sister. "Ally, you're a genius!"

CHAPTER SIX

"Sparkles?" Ally asked the next morning, as she stood in front of the vanity. Their bedroom was littered with outfits, makeup, and shoes. They had slept late—it was almost noon.

"Mmm, too risky." Melanie tried on a hat. "How's this?"

"Nix," Ally said. "Blocks your face."

"Girls!" Jeremy called from downstairs. "We're going to lose our lunch reservation!"

They ignored him. "I've got to hand it to you, Ally," Melanie said. "If we pull this off..."

Just then the phone rang.

"You get it," Ally said nervously.

"No, you!" Melanie said. She felt little flutters of excitement in her stomach.

Ally picked up the phone. "Yes?" She listened for a moment. "We'll be right down." She slammed down the phone and looked at Melanie. "Show time."

The girls raced down the stairs and out the front

door. When they saw the two French boys waiting at the gate on their mopeds, they slowed down, put on their sunglasses, and tried to act casual.

Each boy held a big bouquet of flowers. They recognized Melanie and Ally and smiled.

"Delivery for Melanie Porter," said the taller boy. Today he was wearing a gray T-shirt and jeans.

"That's me," Melanie said, taking the flowers with a smile. *I love the way my name sounds with a French accent!* she thought.

"Livraison pour Allison Porter," said the boy with the light hair. He wore an off-white jacket over a black T-shirt.

"Oui," Ally said. "Je m'appelle Ally."

"Vous parlez Français?" the boy asked as he handed her the flowers. Melanie was pretty sure that meant "Do you speak French?"

"Oui," Ally said, sweetly.

"I am Michel," the darker boy said, smiling at Melanie.

"Jean," said the other one. "It's nice to feed you."

Huh? Melanie thought.

"He means 'Nice to meet you,'" Michel said.

"Between his English and your French, you'll never have a fight," Melanie whispered to Ally.

"I have a great idea," Ally said, her eyes

sparkling. "Why don't you guys come to lunch with us?"

"Awful!" Jean said.

"I think he means 'awesome,'" Michel explained.

Jeremy came toward them impatiently. "Girls, I've been waiting for you. . . ." He broke off when he noticed the boys. "Who are they?" he demanded.

"Jean and Michel," Ally said.

"They're coming to lunch with us," Melanie added brightly.

The two girls walked over to the limousine. Jean and Michel hopped on their mopeds to follow.

"Wait!" Jeremy called. "I don't think—"

"Hurry, Jeremy," Ally called back to him. "We don't want to lose our reservation."

Melanie suppressed a giggle.

Jeremy's face was red with irritation as he climbed into the car.

Moments later they reached the restaurant. It was on a boat on the river. "Cool!" Melanie said.

The restaurant was superfancy, with three forks and two spoons at every place setting. They had a table next to the railing. When the boys came in, Jean sat next to Ally, and Michel sat next to Melanie. Jeremy sat at the end of the table, looking bored.

"Jean's father owns a flower shop," Michel said

to Melanie. "During spring break, we deliver flowers for him so we can make money to buy new instruments for our band. But he won't mind if we take a few hours off."

"You have a band?" Melanie said, leaning forward. Too cool!

Before Michel could answer, a busboy came and poured bottled water into their glasses.

"Doesn't anybody drink regular water here?" Melanie asked. "Like from a sink?"

"Only if you want to be, how you say, talking to Ralph on the big white phone," Michel said.

"Yuck," Melanie said.

"If only the ambassador would read my paper about clean water…." Jeremy mumbled.

On the other side of the table, Ally and Jean were having a harder time communicating—not that it seemed to bother them at all, Melanie noticed.

"Do you like your school?" Ally asked loudly, as if she were talking to someone hard of hearing.

"When the rain comes I am sad," Jean answered.

Ally looked confused. "Okay. Maybe we'd better stick to French. Qu'est-ce que t'aimes lire?"

"Quoi?" Jean said.

"What?" Ally said.

They stared blankly at each other for a second.

Then they both laughed.

Jeremy was looking more and more bored. "Excuse me while I use the little boys' room," he said abruptly, standing up. He left as the waiter arrived.

"Would the mesdemoiselles care to order?" the waiter asked.

"I'll have the chicken—le poulet demideuil, sauce on the side, s'il vous plaît," Ally said.

"You cannot get sauce on the side," the waiter said, frowning.

"Why not?" Ally asked innocently.

"Why not?" the waiter sputtered. "Because Chef Zingaro will not allow it!"

Jean leaped up and spoke angrily to the waiter in French. The waiter's face turned practically purple. He turned and stormed away.

"Wow! What did Jean say?" Melanie asked Michel.

"He said, 'How dare you talk to this beautiful girl that way?'" Michel explained. "And 'Chef Zingaro is the rear end of a flying baboon.'"

"That's the nicest thing anyone's ever done for me," Ally said, her cheeks turning pink.

Jean smiled. "It was anything," he said.

"You mean 'nothing,'" Ally corrected him.

Michel gestured around them with disgust. "This is not Paris," he said. "Come with us! We'll show you the real Paris."

Ally and Melanie looked at each other. What an offer!

"Should we?" Melanie whispered. It was so tempting!

"Are you kidding? Yes!" Ally exclaimed. "Let's go before Jeremy comes back." She grabbed a pen from her knapsack and wrote on a napkin: "J: MEET YOU IN FRONT OF THE EMBASSY AT FIVE. REMEMBER: LEAVE A GOOD TIP."

Michel and Jean gave the girls spare helmets, helped them onto their mopeds, and they were off!

CHAPTER SEVEN

"Wahoo!" Melanie cried, holding onto Michel's shoulders.

"Yee-haa!" yelled Ally, her arms wrapped snugly around Jean's waist.

As they sped through the city, Michel and Jean pointed out the sights.

"This even beats going to the Spring Fling dance!" Melanie yelled to Ally as they slowed down in front of a boulangerie. They bought two baguettes and then went to the great lawn in front of the Eiffel Tower.

"Photo op," Ally said, digging in her knapsack for her camera. A Swiss tourist took a picture of the four of them, having fake swordfights with the baguettes before eating them.

Then they rode all the way across town and stopped at Notre Dame Cathedral. As they climbed the tower to look at the view, Michel rattled off historical facts about the church. On their way down, Jean walked like the Hunchback and got giggles and stares. Before leaving, they had a tourist take a picture of them making gargoyle faces.

Finally, they ended up outside a beautiful white marble church at the top of a large hill.

"This area is Montmartre," Michel said.

"I love it here!" Melanie said.

The place was crowded with street musicians, painters, and food peddlers. They parked their mopeds and began to walk around. Melanie and Michel went one way, and Ally and Jean went another.

"We've been to so many museums," Melanie said as she and Michel strolled past a portrait painter. "But it's all a blur. I'm not sure I could tell the *Mona Lisa* from the Lisa Simpson."

Michel laughed. "Tourists race through the Louvre at fifty miles an hour," he said. "You can't appreciate anything that way. It's better to look at one painting and really see it."

As they walked past an artist painting the Seine, Michel grabbed Melanie's arm. "Wait. What's the hurry?" he said. "See how the artist uses light to capture the emotion of the river?"

Melanie stopped and really looked at the painting. "Wow," she said, amazed. "These colors are what we *wish* we saw every day."

"Exactly," Michel agreed. "It's not supposed to be realistic. It's emotional. That's what art is really about—how you feel when you look at it."

"It's beautiful," Melanie said, studying it some more. She wondered if Ally was also getting a crash course in art appreciation.

Not quite. Ally and Jean were on a bench, eating crêpes that they had bought from a street vendor.

"Now this is *real* French food," Ally said as she chewed.

"Don't they food you at the embassy?" Jean asked.

"Um, yeah, they 'food' us," Ally said between bites. "But not with anything we can recognize."

"You are a funny girl," Jean said, laughing.

An hour later, the four of them met up again under a tree.

"This has been the coolest day," Ally said. "I can't believe all the distance we covered."

"Mopeds are great," Michel said.

"Well, thanks for showing us around," Melanie said. "We've had a great time."

"Time—oh my gosh!" Ally said. Her stomach did a flip-flop. "What time is it?"

"Four forty-five," said a passing tourist.

"We're supposed to be back at the embassy by

five," Melanie said, her eyes wide. "We promised Jeremy in our note."

"We'll never make it!" Ally said. "We're miles away!"

"Never say never," said Michel, leading them back toward the mopeds. Within seconds, they were speeding downhill. They dodged in and out of rush-hour traffic. Ally held tight to Jean's shoulders, squeezing her eyes shut as they zipped around buses and trucks.

They pulled up across the street from the embassy just as they heard a clock strike five. Ally spotted Jeremy, waiting outside the gates and glancing at his watch.

"Meet us tomorrow at two o'clock at the Pont Alexandre," Michel called as the girls hurried toward the gates.

"Okay!" they yelled back.

"I've been worried sick about you all day!" Jeremy sputtered angrily as they ran up. "You've given me no choice but to tell the ambassador what you've been up to today."

Ally rolled her eyes. Didn't he ever loosen up?

"Good idea," Melanie said. "I'm sure Grandpa won't be *too* upset to find out that you let us run around town all day with two boys."

45

"French boys," Ally said.

"Teenage French boys," Melanie added.

Jeremy looked defeated. Ally felt a twinge of sympathy. Didn't he know better than to go up against two teenage girls?

"See you at dinner, J-man," Ally said, as she and Melanie hurried into the embassy.

"So, what did you learn today, girls?" Grandpa Edward asked at dinner.

"Did you know that Notre Dame has an excellent support system of flying buttresses?" Melanie said, trying to ignore the smell of frog legs. "The builders practically invented the Gothic style of architecture in the twelfth century. Could you pass the salt, please?"

Jeremy's mouth dropped open.

"Yeah," said Ally. "The place took two hundred years to build. I guess they weren't in much of a hurry. Salad dressing, please, Jeremy." When he didn't respond, Ally waved her hands in front of his face. "Earth to the J-man."

"Uh, right, sure, dressing," Jeremy murmured.

"Bravo, girls," Grandpa Edward said, sounding impressed. "You have indeed learned something today."

"Yeah, and we owe it all to Jeremy," said Ally. She winked at their confused chaperone.

Later in their room, Melanie and Ally tried to think of a way to meet the boys the following day.

"What we need is a diversion for Jeremy," Melanie said as she sat on her bed. "We should try to stay on his good side."

A slow grin spread across Ally's face. She'd just come up with a fabulous idea. It was so perfect she could hardly even believe it.

"What we need is...a supermodel," she said, holding up a beautiful photograph of Brigitte in the fashion magazine she was reading. "Where did Brigitte say her fashion shoot was?"

"The Jardin du Luxembourg," Melanie said.

"Then that's where we need to go tomorrow morning," Ally said, smiling. "*After* we sneak into Jeremy's room and change the schedule."

CHAPTER EIGHT

"So, J-man, what are we doing today?" Ally asked as she climbed into the limousine. She was wearing a white skirt, a green-and-orange tank top, and barrettes to match. Melanie had on a white sundress and a pink bandanna.

Jeremy looked at the itinerary. "Ten o'clock, the Rodin..." He did a double-take. "Jardin du Luxembourg? That's strange. I could have sworn..."

"Jardin du Luxembourg please, Jacques," Melanie said trying to keep a straight face. Their plan had worked—so far.

After driving down narrow streets lined with shops, Jacques dropped them off in front of the Palais du Luxembourg. Behind it were the gardens.

"Pretty park," Ally said, looking around. They were walking along a path lined with high hedges.

"Bigger than I expected," Melanie said. She wondered how they'd ever find Brigitte's photo shoot.

"My allergies are thrilled," Jeremy muttered,

pulling out his handkerchief. He let out a giant sneeze.

Melanie suddenly caught a glimpse of lights and cameras a little distance away. "Let's go this way," she said, trying not to sound too eager.

They walked toward the shoot. Sure enough, a moment later they spotted Brigitte in front of a cluster of lights, wearing a sleek black gown. "Hey, Mel," Ally said in a casual voice. "Isn't that the supermodel we met at the café?"

Jeremy tore his gaze away from Brigitte long enough to shoot an annoyed glance at the girls. "Right," he said sarcastically. "You girls are friends with a supermodel. Sure."

"That's a wrap, folks," the photographer said. "See you back here at three."

Brigitte spotted Melanie and Ally and waved. "What a nice surprise," she said, approaching them. Jeremy looked stunned as the supermodel kissed each girl on both cheeks.

"Brigitte, this is Jeremy Bluff," Melanie said. She pushed a wide-eyed Jeremy toward Brigitte. "Special assistant to our grandfather, the U.S. ambassador to France."

"Nice to meet you, Mr. Bluff," Brigitte said with a dazzling smile.

"Call me...um...uh..." Jeremy stammmered.

"Jeremy," Ally said.

"Right." Jeremy looked embarrassed.

"You've got an exciting career, Jeremy," Brigitte said. "I've always been interested in foreign diplomacy."

"Really?" Jeremy said, regaining some confidence. "It's a fascinating and complex field."

"I did postgraduate work in international relations at Harvard," Brigitte said.

"Postgraduate?" Jeremy said, looking slightly dazed.

"Oui," said Brigitte. "I did my masters on the Middle East peace talks."

Jeremy's eyes lit up. "Hey, my first posting was in Saudi Arabia!"

Ally and Melanie beamed at each other. "It's working!" Melanie whispered.

They spent the rest of the morning wandering around the gardens. They watched some old men play a game called boules, navigated toy sailboats around a pond, and fed the birds. Melanie and Ally led the way, while Jeremy and Brigitte lagged behind, talking and laughing.

"I hope he's not boring her with all that Clean Water Treaty stuff," Melanie said.

"I guess having clean water isn't such a bad thing to be concerned about, Mel," Ally said.

Melanie sneaked another glimpse behind her. "Well, Brigitte seems to be buying it," she said, "which is all that's important."

"You're right," said Ally. "And it's about time for Phase Two of our plan."

The girls stopped and waited for Brigitte and Jeremy to catch up with them.

"So, uh, Jeremy," Melanie said. "I hate to interrupt, but Ally and I thought it might be fun to go to the Pont Alexandre at two o'clock."

"The Pont Alexandre?" Jeremy asked, looking suspicious.

"You know—the bridge built for the 1900 Exhibition," Ally said. She'd read up on it in their guidebook that morning. "It presents Paris at its grandest."

"There wouldn't be any boys there, by any chance?" Jeremy asked.

"You've met boys?" Brigitte said. "Wow, you girls don't waste any time."

Melanie and Ally couldn't hold back smiles. They knew Brigitte understood.

"Sorry. It's not on your grandfather's agenda," Jeremy said stubbornly.

"But Jeremy," Ally pleaded. "If we don't show up, Jean and Michel will think we stood them up."

"Yeah. And then what will they think of Americans?" Melanie added.

"What kind of diplomat are you?" Ally said.

"Yes, Jeremy, what kind are you?" Brigitte teased.

"Apparently, the kind that caves in," Jeremy said with a little sigh. Then he smiled.

"Yeah! Girl power!" Melanie and Ally shouted, giving Brigitte high fives.

Jacques dropped them off at the Pont Alexandre at 1:55. The walkway along the river was crowded with painters selling their artwork, food vendors, and tourists.

"Years ago, Paris used to hold a yearly swimming competition here," Jeremy said as they waited for the boys. "But it was canceled because the river Seine was so polluted."

"I wish I was passionate about my work, the way you are," Brigitte said. "But modeling is just a job."

"Just a job?" Ally looked shocked.

"Next year, I'm going back to grad school to get my Ph.D. in international relations," Brigitte went on.

"Wow," Melanie said. Sneaking a glance at

Jeremy, she could tell that he was impressed, too. More than impressed, actually. He looked as if he was falling for Brigitte in a big way!

Then Melanie saw Jean and Michel coming toward them, each with a rose in hand.

"Good to see you guys again!" Jeremy called in a friendly voice. He turned to the girls. "Brigitte has to be back at three," he said, "so let's meet back here at two forty-five."

"No problem," Melanie said, not daring to look at Ally. The plan was working better than they could have hoped!

They broke into three couples and set off.

"Do you ever spend time with your grandfather?" Michel asked Melanie as they paused to watch a painter at work.

"Not much," Melanie said. "He's always busy. He thinks we're a nuisance."

"Ah, oui," Michel said.

"It seems that no matter what we do, we can't please him," Melanie said. She sighed and glanced up at Michel. "Know what I mean?"

"Absolutely." Michel leaned against the stone wall. "I can't seem to please my father, either. He's a butcher, and he wants me to take over his business one day. He thinks my music is a waste of time."

"But you can't stop playing your music," Melanie said.

Michel shrugged. "I told him it was important to me. He said, 'You know what's important? A nice filet mignon—that's what's important.'"

Melanie laughed. "I guess it's the same in every country. Adults just don't understand kids."

"Luckily, we have each other," Michel said, taking Melanie's hand.

Melanie sighed again, this time from happiness. The feeling of Michel's hand on hers was so wonderful!

Meanwhile, on the other end of the bridge, Jean and Ally were watching a street performance.

"Okay, Jean," Ally said, "repeat after me: 'That geek is a total freak show.'"

"Zat gik is a total frik show," Jean recited back to her.

"That's great," Ally said, laughing. "A few more key phrases and you're ready for junior high in California."

"American girls like to laugh," Jean said. "Parisian girls are like zees." He put on a snooty expression. "But American girls are like zees." He did a Valley Girl imitation. "Bahn jure—ohmygod!" He pretended to flip his hair back, grinning.

"Stop!" Ally cried. She was laughing so hard she had to hold her stomach. "Stop it! You're killing me!"

"Oh, that would be very sad," Jean said softly. He took her hand. "I like you too much to let that happen."

Before they knew it, it was time to go. When they reached the limousine, the boys kissed the girls' hands.

"We have to work tomorrow," Michel said, "but we'd like to take you out for dinner."

"Great!" said Melanie happily.

"We come at hate," Jean said.

"You mean *eight*." Ally corrected him. "Great!"

They joined Jeremy, who had just put Brigitte in a taxi. He had a goofy grin on his face. "I'm having dinner with her at eight tomorrow night," he said, dreamily.

"I'd say we've done you a pretty big favor, Dr. J," Melanie said, linking her arm with his. "Finding you a supermodel girlfriend and all."

"I wonder how you'll ever repay us," Ally said.

Jeremy looked at the girls with alarm.

"Don't worry, J," Melanie said. "We already have a plan."

CHAPTER NINE

"Did you get it?" Ally whispered. It was about nine o'clock that night. She and Melanie were in the kitchen in their nightshirts.

"Got it," Jeremy said, handing Ally a large white bag. Then he turned to go.

"Wait. Not so fast, J-man," Melanie said. We have to make sure it's all there."

They watched as Ally reached into the bag and pulled out what was inside. "Two Big Macs, two large fries," she said, satisfied.

The girls had asked to be excused from dinner that night. Luckily, their grandfather hadn't asked them why.

"Where's my chocolate shake?" Melanie asked.

"Give me a break!" Jeremy said. "I ran out of cash."

Just then, the overhead lights flickered on.

"Aha!" Henri cried, jumping out at them in his nightshirt and nightcap. He glared at the burgers and fries on the counter. "Ze MickeyDonalds in my kitchen! I think I am going to faint."

"We're sorry, Henri," Ally said sincerely. "But we're hungry."

"Have you ever even tried a fast food burger and fries?" Melanie asked him.

"Of course not!" Henry said, shuddering. "I was trained at le Cordon Bleu. I do not eat ze fast food."

"You're too stuck in your ways," Melanie said. "You have to be more open-minded."

"Me? It is you Americans who are not open-minded."

Melanie raised her eyebrows. "Okay, Henri," she said. "I'll try one of your concoctions if you'll try one of ours." She waved a Big Mac in front of his face.

"It's a deal," Henri said. He took out a dish from the refrigerator and set it in front of Melanie. "Quail eggs with artichokes."

Melanie wrinkled her nose. Ally grinned. *I'm glad* she's *the one who made the deal!* she thought.

Ally unwrapped the Big Mac and poured some fries on the wrapper. "Big Mac with fries," she announced. She shook her head as she saw Henri reaching toward the silverware drawer. "And you have to eat it with your hands."

Henri made a face.

Jeremy counted to three. Then he and Ally watched as Melanie and Henri each took bites.

"Hmmm. Not bad," Melanie said, raising her eyebrows.

Henri took a second bite of the Big Mac, and shoved a fry in after it. "You see," he finally said. "My palate is too refined for this." He took another large bite of the burger and chased it with a handful of fries.

"Try this, Henri." Ally gave him some ketchup.

Henri dipped a French fry in the ketchup. He took a tiny bite. A surprised expression spread over his face. "Mmmm," he murmured. "I had no idea what I was missing!"

When he'd finished everything, he pointed to the second bag of fries. "May I?" he asked, and wolfed them down, too, along with the second Big Mac.

Then Ally realized what had just happened. "Hey, that was our dinner!"

"I'll take you out," Jeremy said. "I need to get more money. Besides, now *I'm* craving a Big Mac."

"All right!" Melanie said. She and Ally ran up to get dressed.

After a meal at McDonalds, Melanie, Ally, and Jeremy walked along the Champs-Élysées, milkshakes in hand. It was a beautiful night.

"Thanks for the Mickey D's, J-man," Ally said.

"I'd forgotten how good it is," Jeremy said. They sat on a bench.

"So, how come Grandpa Edward makes you so miserable?" Melanie asked after a minute.

"Yeah," Ally said. "Why do you stick around the embassy if you hate it so much?"

Jeremy sighed. "I don't hate it," he said. "I'm just frustrated. I want your grandfather to promote me to a policy position. But I've been there three years and I still can't get him to take my ideas about the clean water treaty seriously."

"No offense, Jeremy, but—" Ally began.

"Shoot," Jeremy said, raising his eyebrows.

"Around us you're bossy and stuff, but around Grandpa you act like a...a..." She paused, trying to figure out how to say it in a way that wouldn't hurt his feelings.

"Chicken," Melanie finished for her. "You've just got to stand up for yourself."

Jeremy was silent.

"You know something, Mel?" Ally said slowly. "Maybe we should follow the same advice."

Yeah, she added to herself. *Maybe we should stand up to Grandpa Edward, too. Maybe we should just tell him to back off and not be so strict with us.*

As they began walking back to the embassy, she tried to picture herself and Melanie having that kind of conversation with their grandfather. But all she could picture was his ferocious scowl.

"Yeah, right!" she muttered. "Maybe in the next lifetime!"

CHAPTER TEN

"What in the blazes is this?" Grandpa Edward shouted early the next morning.

Melanie and Ally flung open their bedroom door and hurried downstairs. They peeked through the study door and saw their grandfather staring down at his breakfast tray.

"A French fry, Monsieur," Henri said, smiling. "I thought you'd like fries with your eggs for a change. Bon appétit." As Henri left the study, he and François exchanged high fives.

"The entire staff has gone batty," Grandpa Edward muttered. He popped a fry into his mouth and chewed it, scowling.

After their own breakfast of eggs and fries, Melanie and Ally headed out to the courtyard, where they found Jeremy waiting by the limousine.

"What's on the schedule for today?" Ally asked him.

"Schedule?" Jeremy repeated. He ripped the typed sheet into shreds. "Anything you like."

Melanie looked at Ally. She knew her twin had the exact same idea she had. When you had a dinner date with an adorable French boy, there was only one thing to do....

"Let's go shopping!" Melanie and Ally yelled together.

"I don't do shopping," Jeremy said, "but..."

"I do!" Brigitte said, poking her head out of the car window.

"Cool!" Ally said, flinging the door open.

"It's not every day we can go shopping with a supermodel in Paris!" Melanie said.

Brigitte had Jacques drop them off on a street with supertrendy cool boutiques. There, the three of them tried on skirts, shoes, scarves, earrings, and even socks. And they took a lot of pictures. When they were finally done shopping, Brigitte took them to her favorite restaurant, which served the best sundaes on the planet.

Each twin had found the perfect dress to wear to dinner that evening. Melanie's was red with spaghetti straps. Ally's was a pink-and-blue pastel pattern with spaghetti straps. They also each got a pair of high-heeled sandals.

"You're going to look fab in your new clothes," Brigitte told them on the way back to the embassy.

Melanie thanked her, feeling a little guilty. She and Ally had agreed not to tell Brigitte about their dinner dates. Brigitte might tell Jeremy, and Jeremy might feel he had to tell Grandpa Edward. It was better not to risk it.

Since Grandpa Edward was out at a dinner meeting, no one made a fuss about the girls' not being at dinner. They rested for an hour before getting dressed for their dates.

"How should we sneak out?" Melanie asked, as she helped Ally with her zipper.

"The delivery entrance in the kitchen," Ally said. "I just hope Henri is gone by then."

When they were ready, they stood side by side in front of the vanity mirror.

"Now that you're wearing makeup, Mel, we really look alike," Ally said.

"Yeah, well—it's part of the true test," Melanie reminded her.

"Yep," Ally said. "Can Michel and Jean tell us apart now that we're both dressed up?"

"If they can't, it wasn't meant to be," Melanie said.

They looked at each other nervously. Then they tiptoed down the hall, high heels in hand. The house was quiet, and the kitchen was empty.

"We did it!" Ally said, when they got outside.

"Piece of cake," Melanie said, trying to sound casual.

Michel and Jean were waiting just outside the gates. They both wore black shirts and blazers, and Jean sported a beret. Melanie shook her head in amazement. Talk about good-looking!

The boys spotted the girls and began to walk toward them. But Melanie was horrified to see Michel heading for Ally instead of her!

"No!" Ally gasped softly. "They can't fail the true test!"

But then Michel crossed smoothly in front of Jean, and Jean just as smoothly changed his direction. Michel stood in front of Melanie, and Jean in front of Ally.

Melanie let out her breath. They passed! It *was* meant to be!

"Ally!" Jean said. He kissed Ally on both cheeks in the French style.

"Melanie!" Michel said, doing the same.

"How French!" Ally gushed.

"We are so glad you were able to sneak out," Michel said.

Melanie's reply caught in her throat as a figure stepped out of the shadows.

It was Jeremy. He was followed by Brigitte, who wore a red silk dress.

"You almost made it," Jeremy said. He looked at the girls, shook his head sadly, and pulled out his cell phone.

"Oh, no!" Ally gasped.

Melanie stared pleadingly at Jeremy. Was he really going to rat them out to their grandfather?

CHAPTER ELEVEN

Ally's heart fell all the way down into her sandals as Jeremy began to dial.

"Michel and Jean are just taking us to dinner," Melanie said. "Please, Jeremy! This is so important to us."

"'Allo, François," Jeremy said into the phone. "Please tell the ambassador..." He paused and glanced at the girls one more time.

Ally and Melanie both stared back pleadingly at him.

Jeremy bit his lip. "Tell him that I've taken the girls out for ice cream."

Yes! Ally threw up her arms in a silent cheer. "Thank you," she mouthed at Jeremy.

"J-man, you're pretty cool after all," Melanie said.

"Where are you taking them?" Brigitte asked Michel and Jean when Jeremy had hung up.

"Our favorite restaurant," Michel said.

"Oui. Secret place," Jean said.

"Be back here in three hours," Jeremy said, "And don't be late. I'm holding you boys personally responsible. Comprenez-vous?"

"You have to worry," Jean said, helping Ally onto his moped.

"He means 'you *don't* have to worry'," Michel said, nudging his friend. He helped Melanie onto his own moped, and they were off.

They pulled up alongside a dark building and parked. Melanie looked around, puzzled.

"I thought we were going to your favorite restaurant," Ally said.

"We are," Jean said, leading them up a fire ladder on the outside wall.

When they reached the roof, Melanie and Ally gasped in amazement. There, spread out below them, was a magnificent view of Paris! The Eiffel Tower sparkled against the night sky.

"Welcome to Restaurant Jean-Michel," Jean said, gesturing toward a picnic blanket set with candles, food, and a boom box playing swing music.

"It's so romantic!" Ally said.

"This rocks!" Melanie added.

"We cooked it ourselves," Michel told them proudly.

The food was delicious. After they ate, Michel led Melanie to the edge of the roof.

"This view takes my breath away," Melanie told him.

"Are you feeling sick?" Michel sounded worried.

Melanie giggled. "No, that's just an expression," she explained.

Michel was silent for a moment. "Melanie," he finally said. "Our band, the Videoheads, will be playing tomorrow night at a school dance, and..."

"Yes?" Melanie asked, feeling a little breathless.

"I wish very much that you could come. Would you like to go with me?" Michel asked.

Would she? "Of course!" Melanie said. "You know, I used to think going to Disney World when I was nine was the best day of my life, but now..." She smiled into his eyes. "I had no idea life could be so amazing."

Michel leaned toward her. His eyes began to close, and she knew he was about to kiss her. Her heart thudded so loudly she wondered if he could hear it.

As they sat on the blanket, Jean asked Ally to go to the dance with him.

"That sounds awesome," she said happily. "I'd love to!"

"I am happy for to go you," Jean said.

"Wow," Ally said, laughing. "I actually understood you!"

She bit into an éclair. Jean reached over to wipe a dollop of chocolate off her nose. For a moment they gazed into each other's eyes.

Then Jean bent forward. Ally caught her breath.

But just as their lips were about to meet...

"Eh, les gamins, qu'est-ce que vous faîtes?"

A bright flashlight beam swept across the roof. Ally gulped.

Behind the light was a police officer.

The officer reached up and pulled Jean's jacket off the low wall at the edge of the roof. Under the jacket was a sign.

"What does it say?" Melanie asked curiously.

"No loitering," Michel told her.

"Violators will be executed," Jean added.

"Prosecuted," Michel corrected him.

"I'm not sure which is worse," Ally said, giving Melanie a doomed look.

"Come on," Michel said. "We have to go to the police station." He added miserably, "I think we are in big trouble."

CHAPTER TWELVE

"Allison, Melanie, I'm very disappointed in you," Grandpa Edward said.It was after midnight, and Melanie, Ally, Jeremy, and Brigitte were all in Grandpa Edward's study. After four hours in the police station, the police officer had finally driven Melanie and Ally back to the embassy.

"I am the U.S. ambassador to France," Grandpa Edward went on. "I cannot have my granddaughters hauled into police headquarters. Nor do I want them wandering around Paris with two delinquent French boys!"

"How can you say that? You don't even know them," Melanie protested.

"Sir, if I might—" Jeremy began.

"I'll deal with you later, Jeremy," Grandpa Edward said shortly.

"You'll deal with me now, sir," Jeremy said, surprising everyone. "I can't stand here and listen to you criticize these girls unfairly. Ally and Melanie are terrific kids who came to Paris hoping to have fun. They met two boys who introduced them to the crazy, romantic Paris you once knew—and that I'm just discovering." He winked at Brigitte. Then he went on. "Sir, these girls are smart and full of life. You'd find this out for yourself if you took the time to get to know them."

Go, Jeremy! Melanie wanted to cheer.

"Mr. Bluff!" Grandpa Edward said stiffly.

"And one more thing," Jeremy said. "I gave you my paper on the Clean Water Treaty a week ago, but I can see you have no interest in it." He took a deep breath. "So, sir, with all due respect...I quit."

Everyone gasped.

"No, Jeremy, you can't!" Ally exclaimed.

"Not because of us," Melanie said.

"You girls have given me the courage to do what I should have done months ago," Jeremy said. He gave each of them a kiss on the cheek. Then he took Brigitte's arm and headed out.

There was a long silence. Then Grandpa Edward turned to his granddaughters. "You are forbidden to see those boys again!" he barked. "Is that understood?"

Stand up to him! Melanie told herself. *Tell him it's not understood at all!*

But she couldn't do it. She didn't have the nerve.

71

"Yes, sir," she mumbled at last.

"Yes, sir," Ally echoed meekly.

The girls lay in bed, unable to sleep.

Ping! Something bounced off the window.

Could it be? Ally wondered. "Mel?" she said.

"I heard it," Melanie said.

The girls raced to the balcony and looked down.

"Bonsoir, ma crème brulée," Jean whispered up from the courtyard. "We're sorry for all the trouble!"

"Don't worry," Ally said. "Except…"

"We have some bad news," Melanie said. "We can't go with you to the dance."

"You guys can ask someone else," Ally said with a lump in her throat. "We'll understand."

"Never," said Michel. "Either we go with Melanie and Ally Porter, or we go alone."

"Right!" Jean said, too loudly.

"Hello? Is someone out there?" The girls recognized François's voice.

The boys blew the girls kisses and hurried away.

Melanie and Ally watched glumly as they disappeared through the gates. "Don't forget us," Ally whispered.

CHAPTER THIRTEEN

"The water's mercury content..." Ally read aloud, frowning. She was holding a copy of Jeremy's paper on the Clean Water Treaty. She and Melanie had found it in his room when they went to see if he had really left. He had.

"...parts per billion..." Melanie continued. "Yikes!"

The two girls lay across Melanie's bed. They could hear pots and pans clanging in the kitchen as Henri and his staff prepared for the banquet that night.

"Do you understand this stuff?" Ally asked.

"Not a word," Melanie said.

There was a knock on the door.

"Come in," Ally called, tucking the paper under Melanie's covers.

Grandpa Edward came in, holding two big boxes. "Packing already?" he asked gently.

"Thought we'd get started," Ally said, looking at the floor. They hadn't spoken to their grandfather since the night before, and she didn't much feel like speaking to him now.

"Mind if I sit?" Grandpa Edward asked.

The girls shrugged. He sat down.

"Girls, I must apologize," he said.

Ally glanced up, shocked.

"I should have spent more time with you this week," he said. When Melanie and Ally remained silent, he continued. "I understand that Paris has a certain glamour—I met your grandmother here, you know."

"Really?" Ally asked, curious in spite of herself.

"At the end of World War Two, I was a soldier stationed here in Paris," Grandpa Edward said, a dreamy look in his eyes. "Your grandmother was a nurse. When the war was over, I was afraid we'd never see each other again. I'd only known her a few weeks, but I spent every franc I had to take her on a boat ride down the Seine. As we passed under the Pont Neuf, I proposed to her. She said yes—and we were together forty-five years."

"Wow," Melanie said. "You never told us that story, Grandpa."

"Well, I guess we haven't done much talking in the past, have we?" Grandpa Edward said. He sounded a little sad.

Ally didn't know what to say. It was so nice to have their grandfather open up to them. If only he hadn't waited until their trip was almost over!

"Oh, before I forget," Grandpa Edward said, "these are for you." He handed each of them a large box. "Thought you might need a little something to wear to the banquet tonight."

Ally gasped as she opened hers. "Wow, Grandpa!" Inside was a red velvet dress with tiny pearls stitched into star shapes along the neckline and hem.

Melanie's was the same design, but black. "They're beautiful," she said.

Ally tried not to imagine what it would be like to wear that beautiful dress to the dance with Jean.

"It's our last night together, so let's enjoy it and make up for lost time," Grandpa Edward said.

Ally put the dress back in its box and gazed up at him. "Why is this dinner so important to you, Grandpa?"

Grandpa Edward sighed. "Well, let's just say there are people who want me to retire. If they can keep me from getting the Clean Water Treaty signed, I'll have to step down."

"Don't you want to retire?" Melanie asked.

"And do what? I have a lot of fight left in me,"

Grandpa Edward said. Then he left the room.

"So, the Tin Man has a heart after all," Melanie murmured, staring after him.

Melanie couldn't help feeling excited as she and Ally walked slowly down the grand staircase that evening. The dresses looked fabulous, and the high heels they'd bought the day before matched perfectly. The embassy was elegantly decorated, with soft lighting and classical music in the background.

"Melanie, Ally, I'd like to introduce Foreign Minister Monsieur de Beauvoir and his wife, Madame de Beauvoir," Grandpa Edward said.

"Enchanté, mesdemoiselles," said the foreign minister, a balding man in a tuxedo and bow tie. His wife wore a long gown and glittering jewelry.

"Nice to meet you," Melanie said.

"Je suis ravie de faire votre connaissance," Ally said, in perfect French.

"Where did she learn to speak such excellent French, Ambassador?" de Beauvoir asked. "Not in your American schools, I trust." He chuckled in a superior way. Melanie decided she didn't much like him.

François presented a tray of small hamburgers. "A new dish—Le Boeuf Mélanie," he announced, winking at Melanie. Melanie grinned.

De Beauvoir tried one. "Mmm. C'est délicieux," he said. "An absolutely unique creation."

The table was exquisitely set, with the finest crystal and china. Grandpa Edward sat at the head, with de Beauvoir and his wife to his left and Melanie and Ally to his right. There were twenty-five guests in all.

Grandpa Edward and de Beauvoir immediately fell into a serious talk about the Clean Water Treaty.

"We are not convinced this is the best use of our financial resources," de Beauvoir was saying.

"Mel, remember what Grandpa told us about how important this treaty is? We have to help him," Ally whispered.

Melanie was thinking the same thing. But what could they do?

She watched her grandfather take a sip of water. "Hey!" Her eyes widened. "I've got it!" She waved François over and whispered in his ear. Then she and Ally put their heads together as she explained her plan.

Moments later, François poured water into de Beauvoir's glass. The girls watched as de Beauvoir, still deep in conversation, took a sip—and spat it out all over the table.

Everyone gasped in horror. "What is the meaning of this, Edward?" de Beauvoir said, holding up the glass. It was filled with murky brown water.

"I have no idea," Grandpa Edward said angrily. "Who's responsible for this?"

"We are!" Melanie and Ally announced, rising.

"What?" Grandpa Edward exclaimed. "You'd better have an explanation, girls!"

"We do!" Ally turned to her sister. "Take it away, Mel."

"Me?" Melanie said nervously. Suddenly she had a horrible attack of stage fright. Everyone was staring at her!

"Well..." she began. Her voice shook a little. "France has always prided itself on being at the cutting edge of water technology." She thought back to Mr. Harper's social studies lectures. "Napoleon built aqueducts and modern sewers so France would have the most happening water system in the world."

A murmur circled the table.

"I had no idea," Madame de Beauvoir said.

Ally spoke up. "Napoleon understood national pride. Parisians once drank out of public fountains and swam in the Seine for fun..."

"...but now every time we ask for water,"

Melanie continued, "it comes in a bottle, because French water is so polluted. Is this the kind of world we want to live in?" She held up the glass of murky water.

"A world where the mercury content is twenty-seven parts per billion, and it makes you glow in the dark?" Ally added.

"I don't think so!" the twins finished together. "Jinx!" they added, grinning at each other.

"Allison, Melanie," Grandpa Edward said, breaking the jinx.

"Thanks, Grandpa," Melanie said. She gazed around the table. "I ask you—what cost is too high when the people's health and your place in history are at stake?"

There was a moment of silence. Then de Beauvoir smiled. "Edward, I'm afraid your grand-daughters are more persuasive than you are," he said, turning to Melanie and Ally. "Bravo, girls. Your spirit and passion is rarely found in young people these days. You have convinced me to petition my government to sign on to the Clean Water Treaty."

The guests applauded. Melanie felt a glow of triumph.

Grandpa Edward beamed at Melanie and Ally. "François, water for everyone!" he said.

Soon after, the party broke up. As the guests began to leave, Ally and Melanie pulled Grandpa Edward aside. "We're going to go up and finish packing, if it's all right with you," Ally said.

Grandpa Edward raised his eyebrows. "I was under the impression you had a dance to attend," he said, smiling. "Unless you're too tired?"

"No!" Ally and Melanie shouted, breaking into huge grins.

"Jacques is waiting outside," Grandpa Edward said. He put an arm around each of the girls' shoulders. "I think I'll come along for the ride."

CHAPTER FOURTEEN

"How did you know about the dance, Grandpa?" Melanie asked on their way to the school.

"I heard you talking to those boys last night in the courtyard," Grandpa Edward explained.

He pushed a button, and a sunroof slid open.

"Can we?" Ally said, looking up.

Grandpa Edward nodded as the two girls poked their heads out. It felt wonderful.

"Grandpa, you've got to stick your head out," Ally called.

"Yeah," Melanie added. "Paris is totally A-plus at night."

"As ambassador, I can't ride around with my head..." Grandpa Edward began. Then he stopped himself. "Oh, why not!"

He poked his head through the sunroof next to Melanie and Ally.

"Wahoo!" yelled Melanie.

"Wahoo!" yelled Ally

"Wahooooo!" yelled Grandpa Edward.

The air pulsed with music as Melanie and Ally entered the school gym. The dance floor was packed. Onstage, the Videoheads were jamming, with Jean on bass and Michel on guitar. The girls were on their way to the stage when Melanie spotted two familiar figures. "Look!" she said.

"Jeremy! Brigitte!" Ally called, pushing toward them.

"What are you guys doing here?" Melanie demanded.

"This is Jeremy's last chance to chaperone you two before he starts his new job," Brigitte explained.

"What new job?" Ally asked.

"I've been rehired—as the *senior* policy advisor to the American ambassador," Jeremy said proudly.

"Give it up for the J-man!" Melanie cheered. "And for Grandpa Edward, too!"

"We hope you don't mind, but we read your paper," Ally told Jeremy. "Great stuff."

"Ally! Melanie!" Jean and Michel shouted from the stage. The two boys dropped their instruments and rushed toward the girls, leaving the rest of the band to play alone. Melanie felt a huge grin stretch across her face.

"May we have this dance?" Michel asked for both of them.

Michel led Melanie to an open spot and put his arms around her for a slow dance. Melanie leaned against him.

"I wish you didn't have to leave tomorrow," Michel said sadly. "I don't know when I'll see you again."

"When the Videoheads get famous, maybe you'll tour in L.A.," Melanie said. She looked up into his eyes.

"No police will interrupt us this time," he murmured. Then he leaned down, and their lips met in a soft, romantic kiss.

I'm flying! Melanie thought. *This is the greatest feeling!*

A few feet away, Ally and Jean were dancing. "I'll e-mail you every day," Ally promised.

"I'll e-mail you *twice* a day," Jean said.

"Three times a day," Ally said. "That's my final offer."

Jean laughed. "I'll miss you, funny girl." He tilted her chin up with one finger, and kissed her on the lips.

Ally closed her eyes in bliss. *If this is a dream, I don't ever want to wake up!* she thought happily.

*   *   *

The next morning, the girls got up early, dressed in comfortable clothes for the airplane, and finished packing. After a light breakfast, it was time to say their good-byes.

As they came down the grand staircase for the last time, Henri rushed up to them and handed them each a paper bag.

"It's a special pâté appetizer and quiche lorraine for the flight," he said, "and it must be heated to one hundred fourteen degrees or..." His lower lip started to quiver.

Laughing, the girls hugged him.

"I'll miss your flying food," François said as he brought their bags downstairs. "À tout à l'heure, mesdemoiselles."

" À tout à l'heure, François," Ally said.

"A toodle-loo to you, too, François," Melanie said.

Jeremy and Brigitte were waiting in the courtyard. "I guess this is good-bye," Jeremy said.

"Aren't you coming to the airport?" Ally asked.

"No. I am," Grandpa Edward said, poking his head out of one of the limousine windows.

The girls looked at each other in surprise.

"Well, then..." Jeremy said. He sniffed loudly.

"You're not going to get all mushy-gushy on us, are you, J-man?" Melanie asked.

"Yeah," Ally said. "That could kill your rep—big time."

Jeremy smiled and hugged them.

"We'll see you back in the States," Brigitte promised, kissing each girl on both cheeks. Then the girls climbed into the limousine, one on each side of their grandfather.

"To the airport, Jacques," Grandpa Edward said. "We've got a plane to catch."

"*We?*" Melanie said, confused.

"I'm taking a vacation, girls," said Grandpa Edward. "I need to spend some time chilling with my 'A-plus' family."

"Awesome!" Melanie and Ally said together, throwing their arms around their grandfather.

"Jinx!" Grandpa Edward called. He grinned at their expressions. "Let's see...Pallison, Callison, Jelanie, Zelanie. Aah, it's going to be a nice, quiet flight home."

CHAPTER FIFTEEN

Two days later, Melanie and Ally were walking home from school. Each of them was reading a book as they walked.

"It says here that Rome's streets are paved with the history of civilization," Ally said, looking up from her book.

"Africa's grasslands have some of the world's largest herds of elephant, rhinoceros, giraffe, and zebra," Melanie read out loud from her book.

"There are so many amazing places in the world," Ally said, sighing. "How will we see them all?"

Just then, Shane and Kyle rode by on their bicycles. When they saw the girls, they circled back and stopped.

"Hey, Ally," Shane said to Ally.

"Hey, Mel," Kyle said to Melanie.

"Oh, hey, Kyle," Melanie said to Shane, barely glancing up from her book.

"Hi Shane," Ally said to Kyle, flipping a page.

"Uh, that's Kyle, I'm Shane," Shane said. "Hey, do you want to get some frozen yogurt at the mall?"

Ally glanced at Melanie, who shook her head slightly.

"Thanks, but we have homework," Ally said.

"Maybe some other time," Melanie said.

The girls walked away. If they'd looked back, they would have seen Shane and Kyle staring after them in shock—but they didn't look back.

"Now, where were we?" Melanie asked.

"I think it was Africa," Ally said.

They linked arms. "Ally," Melanie said with a smile, "I think this is the beginning of a lifetime of adventures!"

TIME TO PARTY

with Mary-Kate and Ashley

3 Great Videos to Own!

SCHOOL DANCE PARTY

All NEW SCHOOL DANCE PARTY plus Our Music Video. Two Rockin' Episodes.

Greatest Parties

Three Pure-Party Episodes

Hand-Picked by Mary-Kate & Ashley Fans

The Amazing Adventures of MARY-KATE & ASHLEY

Three Amazing Episodes

Hand-Picked by Mary-Kate & Ashley Fans

Outta-site!
marykateandashley.com
Register Now

DUALSTAR VIDEO

mary-kateandashley
Magical Mystery Mall™

Octo

2000

PlaySta

outta site!

marykateandashley.com
Register Now

Check out
the Reading Room on
marykateandashley.com
for an exclusive
online chapter preview
of our upcoming book!

DUALSTAR
PUBLICATIONS